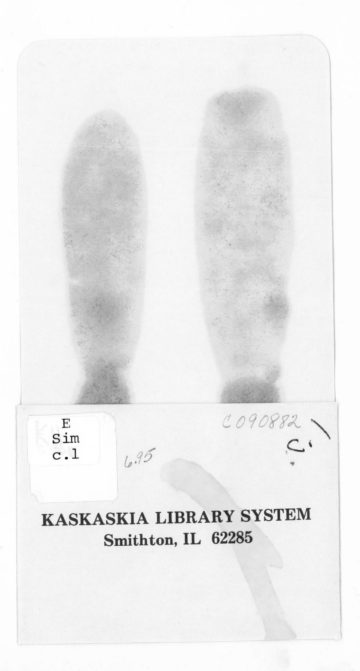

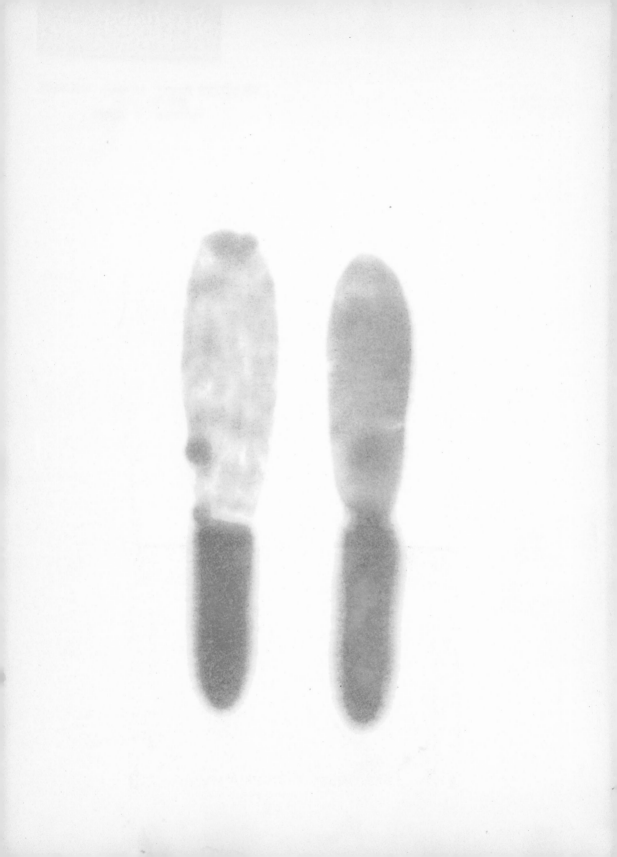

ELLY
THE ELEPHANT

story by Norma Simon
pictures by Stanley Bleifeld

ALBERT WHITMAN & COMPANY, NILES, ILLINOIS

Library of Congress Cataloging in Publication Data

Simon, Norma.
   Elly the elephant.
   Summary: Wendy and her beloved Elly are inseparable
until the toy is left at school one day.
   [1. Toys—Fiction] I. Bleifeld, Stanley, ill.
II. Title.
PZ7.S6053E1 1982   [E]   81-23990
ISBN 0-8075-1970-7 (lib. bdg.)   AACR2

A NOTE ABOUT THIS BOOK

Most people have a toy

teddy bear   or a panda

or a monkey   or a tiger

who lives in their house and is a very special
member of their family. Elly is the elephant who
lives in our house. He is very special to all of us,
but most of all to Wendy. She loves him very
much. When Elly talks in his high, squeaky voice,
it's Wendy talking for him.

Do you tell stories about your special toy friend?
Maybe a grownup and you can write down *your*
stories, just the way Wendy and I did.

This is the way Wendy tells her story of Elly the
Elephant.

Norma Simon

ELLY

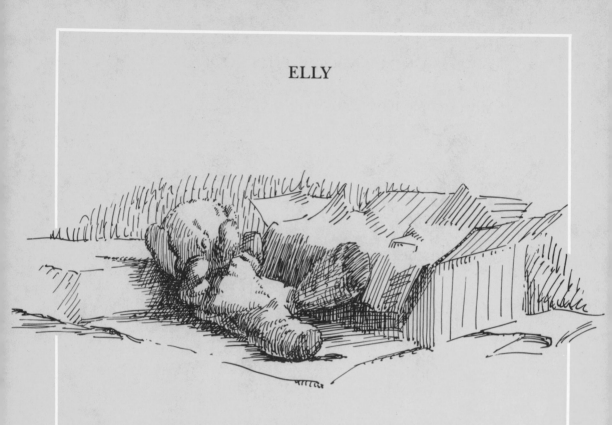

I have a little elephant with red velvet ears,
and he used to be all white.
But I loved him so much,
and I loved him so long,
he's worn out in spots and looks gray,
like a real elephant.
Elly was a present from my Aunt Tess
and my Uncle Austin.
Elly came a long, long way to get to my house.
We loved each other as soon as he came out of the box.
My mama says they made him in a factory.

I want to make a pouch for Elly,
like a kangaroo has.
But I don't have the same fur.
It should be the same fur,
don't you think?
Some day I'll go to the factory
where they make elephants,
and I'll say, "Please give me fur for Elly's pouch."
Then my mama will sew a pouch.

AN ELLY SONG

oom-pah style

I'm El – ly. I'm El – ly. I

like to eat jel – ly. I'm

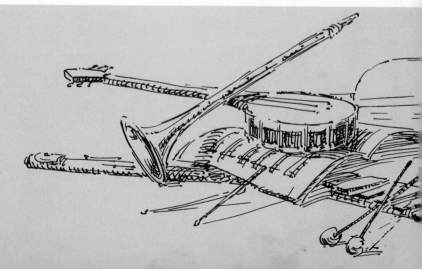

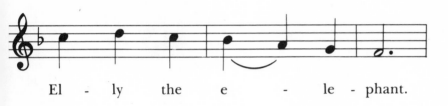

El - ly the e - le - phant.

ELLY HAS ANOTHER BIRTHDAY

I have to wait forever for birthdays,
but Elly is so lucky.
Almost every day
                is a birthday
                              for Elly.

He doesn't grow bigger,
but now he's nine years old.
And whenever he tells me it's his birthday,
we have a party.
When Mama bakes a cake,
just a pretty cake,
Elly says, in his squeaky voice,
    "It's my birthday."
So we put candles on the cake,
and my whole family sings,

      "Happy birthday to you,
       Happy birthday to you,
       Happy birthday, dear Elly,
       Happy birthday to you."

Then we all laugh at silly Elly
with all his birthdays.
But he doesn't get even a little bit bigger.
That's because he's a toy elephant, you know.

AN ELLY SONG

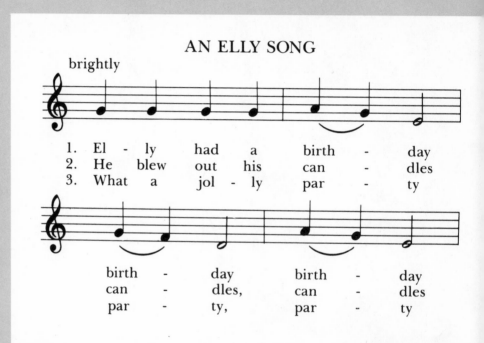

brightly

1. El - ly had a birth - day
2. He blew out his can - dles
3. What a jol - ly par - ty

birth - day   birth - day
can - dles,   can - dles
par - ty,   par - ty

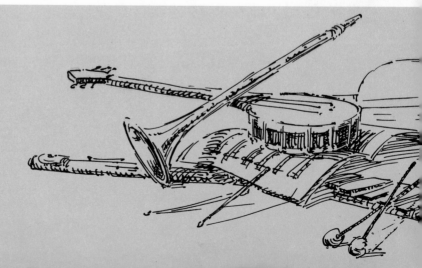

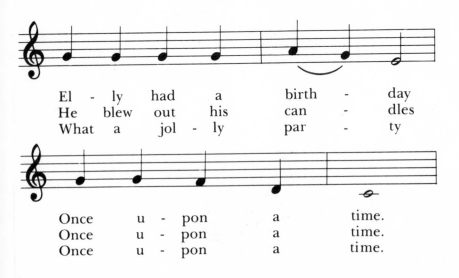

El - ly had a birth - day
He blew out his can - dles
What a jol - ly par - ty

Once u - pon a time.
Once u - pon a time.
Once u - pon a time.

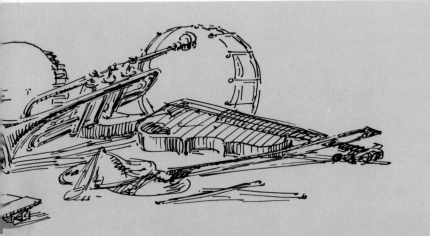

ELLY AND HIS COUSINS

I carry Elly all around
my house.
Wherever I go,

      Elly goes.

Mostly Elly just sits and watches me.
Sometimes I let Elly hold something for me.

One day I couldn't find Elly.

I looked high.
I looked low.
No Elly.

I knew Elly was home.
Where could he be?
Oh,   I forgot all about it.
He was visiting his cousins,
invisible ones,
but Elly said *he* could see them.
When he was all finished
with his visit,
he would come back to me.
That's what Elly said.

I missed Elly
when it started to grow dark.
I called,
"El-ly, are you coming soon?"
Elly was so busy with his cousins,
he didn't hear.
I could hear him squeaking away,
but no Elly.
I washed my hands for supper.
And right in the middle of the bathtub
was Elly.

What a silly place
to visit his cousins!
That's where they were all the time.
I didn't see the cousins.
Just Elly did.
Elly had a happy time visiting
all by himself.

Elly came to supper with me.
He waved goodbye to his cousins in the bathtub.

ELLY AND THE BABY SITTER

My mama didn't think Elly should go to the dentist
because he doesn't have any teeth.
He goes to school with me,
but the dentist's office is a very busy place.
I wanted Elly to come.
But I found a sitter for Elly.
Mary,   my doll,   is a good sitter.
I put out some treats.
I showed Mary where Elly's toys are.
And I kissed Elly goodbye.
He didn't look very happy.
He likes to go with me.

But I said,   "Elly,
sometimes you have to stay with a sitter."

He still looked sad,
so I kissed him again.

I put on my hat.
"Goodbye, Elly.
Goodbye, Mary.
I'll see you later."

The dentist was happy to see me.
He said,   "No cavities today."
He made my teeth shiny.
He gave me a big balloon.
He blew it up himself.
I said,   "Goodbye."
He said,   "See you soon."
And I took my big balloon.

The minute I came in the door,
I knew something was wrong.
Elly was crying
and Mary was talking.
I ran right in with my big balloon.
"Elly,   Elly,   I'm home.
What's the matter, baby?"
Elly stopped crying when he saw me.
He liked my big balloon.

I told my mama,
"See,   I should never listen to you.
Mary says he fussed
all the time I was gone."

"I won't leave you again,   Elly,
I promise,
until you're a great big elephant."
But Elly wasn't listening one bit.
He was watching my big balloon.
Maybe I'll try a sitter again.
Just maybe I will,   just maybe.

AN ELLY SONG

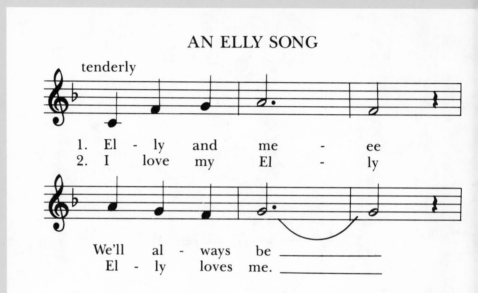

tenderly

1. El - ly   and   me - ee
2. I   love   my   El - ly

We'll   al - ways   be _____
El - ly   loves   me. _____

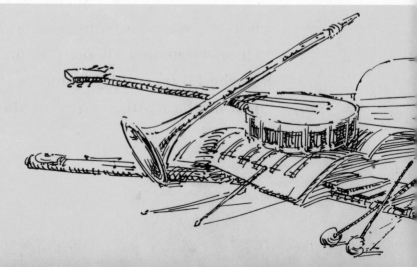

El - ly and me - ee
El - ly and me - ee

We'll al - ways be. _____
We'll al - ways be. _____

THE NIGHT I SLEPT ALONE

One day Elly and I went to school.
We always go to school together.
Some days Elly doesn't want to go to school.

I say,　"Elly, baby,　everybody goes to school.

　　　　And you'll see your friends there.

　　　　And they have such nice toys.

　　　　I'll build a house for you. All right?"

And Elly shakes his head,　　"Yes."

We went into school.

Elly waited for me to undress.

My friend,　　Nancy,　　was waiting for Elly and me.

"Want to help me build a house for Elly?"

"I'll try,"　　Nancy said.

Nancy and I built a big Elly house.

Then we picked it up.

We put all the blocks away

and went to have a juice time.

Mama and I were driving home.
"Elly!   Elly!   I forgot Elly!
Go back for Elly."
Mama turned the car around.
All the children were home.
The school looked empty and quiet.
The teacher looked for Elly.
My mama looked for Elly.

I looked	everywhere.
I called,	"Elllllllly, Elllllllly,"
No Elly.	
Teacher said,	"We'll look again tomorrow."
Mama said,	"I'm sorry, but I'm sure we'll find him tomorrow."
I said,	"Did *you* ever lose an elephant? I want my Elly!"

I didn't like to sleep alone.

I wasn't used to sleeping alone.

Elly always slept with me ever since he came.

I wanted my Elly.
I called my mama.

> She sat by my bed.
> She patted my head.
> She sang me a song.

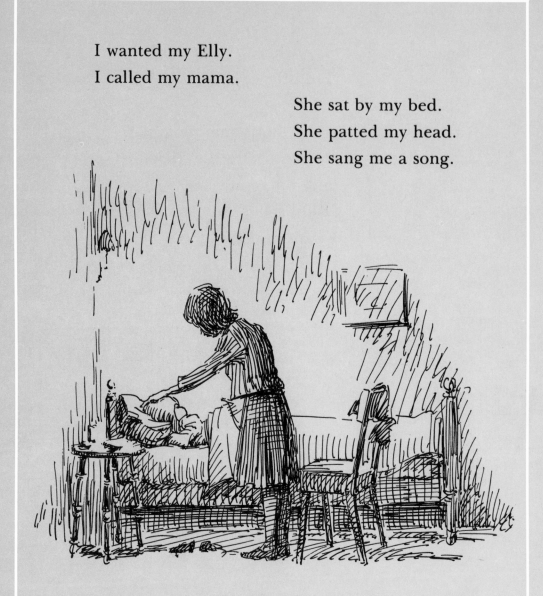

But I wanted my Elly.
I was lonely all night   without Elly.

I dressed myself in the morning

without Elly.

I ate my breakfast

without Elly.

We drove to school

without Elly.

Mama stayed at school
to look for Elly.
That was nice
but I wanted Elly.

We looked on top of everything.

We looked under everything.

We looked behind the blocks.
Other children came to help.
Nancy helped me look.

Everybody looked for a little lost elephant.

And then, when there were no more places to look,
Guess where he was?

Right in the middle of all the dolls!

"Elly, Elly,   THERE YOU ARE!

"Did they take good care of you, Elly?
I'm so happy you're here.
I missed you,   Elly.
I was lonely for you,   Elly.
I'm so happy we're together,   little Elly boy."
My mama was happy.
My teacher was happy.
The children were happy.
Elly was happy.
"My little lost elephant!
I love you,   Elly dear.
And we'll live happily ever after."

THE END

AN ELLY SONG

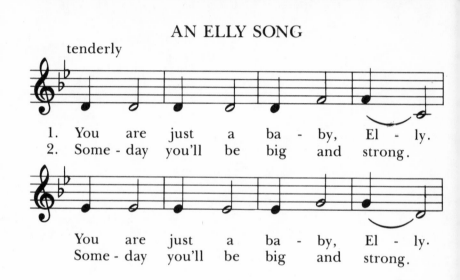

tenderly

1. You are just a ba - by, El - ly.
2. Some - day you'll be big and strong.

You are just a ba - by, El - ly.
Some - day you'll be big and strong.

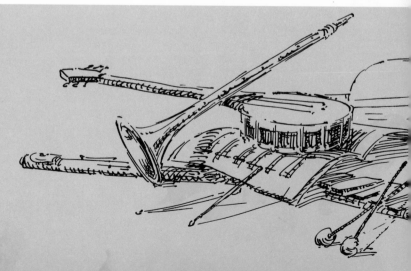

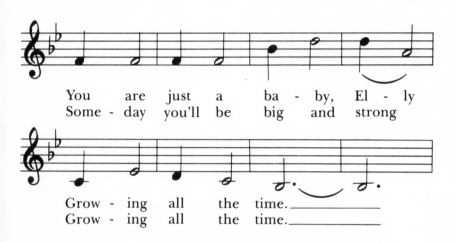

You   are   just   a   ba -   by,   El - ly
Some - day   you'll   be   big   and   strong

Grow - ing   all   the   time._____
Grow - ing   all   the   time._____

NORMA SIMON

In her more than thirty-five books for children, Norma Simon has shown exceptional awareness of children's perceptions and emotions. Her natural sensitivity to children's concerns has been heightened by her studies at the New School for Social Research and the Bank Street College of Education, where she received a master's degree. She has also served as an educational consultant to the Bank Street College and to various companies that produce educational films and television programs for children. Mrs. Simon makes frequent visits to her local grade school, where she spends much time talking with children.

STANLEY BLEIFELD

Since Stanley Bleifeld completed the line drawings for *Elly the Elephant,* he has devoted himself almost exclusively to sculpture. Greatly influenced by Donatello and Rodin, Mr. Bleifeld's works are realistic, energetic, and emotionally powerful. He is concerned with psychological themes and has frequently chosen Biblical subjects, such as the prophecies of the coming of the Messiah, which he portrayed in bas-relief for the Vatican Pavilion at the 1964/65 New York World's Fair. Recently he has been commissioned to do a sculpture for the Naval Monument in Washington, D.C.